For Tim ~ S S

For everyone who has ever had monsters
under their bed, and James,
who scares mine away! ~ C P

LITTLE TIGER PRESS LTD,
an imprint of the Little Tiger Group
1 Coda Studios, 189 Munster Road, London SW6 6AW
Imported into the EEA by Penguin Random House Ireland,
Morrison Chambers, 32 Nassau Street, Dublin D02 YH68
www.littletiger.co.uk

First published in Great Britain 2009
This edition published 2016
Text copyright © Steve Smallman 2009
Illustrations copyright © Caroline Pedler 2009

Steve Smallman and Caroline Pedler have asserted their rights
to be identified as the author and illustrator of this work under
the Copyright, Designs and Patents Act, 1988
A CIP catalogue record for this book is available from the British Library

ISBN 978-1-84869-461-3
Printed in China
LTP/1800/3804/0321
10 9 8 7

There's No Such Thing As MONSTERS!

Steve Smallman
Caroline Pedler

LiTTLE TiGER
LONDON

"I've got my own bedroom, I'm so-o big now!"
sang Little Bear excitedly. Big Bear was excited
too. He had his bedroom all to himself at last.
"Off to bed, dozy head!" chuckled Big Bear.

Little Bear snuggled down and tried
to go to sleep . . . but he couldn't.

Everything felt different. The dark seemed
so much darker without Big Bear there.
Then, as Little Bear peered into the shadows,
he saw . . .

...A monster!

A BIG scaly monster...

all covered in spines, watching
and waiting, and ready to pounce!

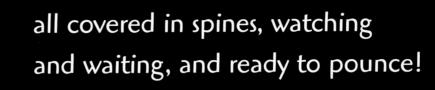

"Big Bear!
Big Bear!"

cried Little Bear.

"There's a spiky monster in my
room and it's coming to get me!"

Big Bear rushed in
and turned on the light.
But there wasn't a monster,
just a floppy old toy on the
back of the chair.

Big Bear put it on his head and
did a silly spiky monster dance.
"Don't be a scaredy bear,
shadows can't hurt
you!" he said.

Little Bear snuggled down and tried to go
to sleep, but it was just too quiet without
Big Bear there. He tried humming a little
song to keep the quiet out. Then he thought,
"What if there's something under my bed –
something that's keeping very still?"

Shhhhhh!

He wriggled nervously over to
the edge, peeked underneath
and saw . . .

...a **monster's tail!**

"Big Bear!
Big Bear!"

squealed Little Bear. "There's a slimy monster
under my bed and it's going to EAT me!"

Big Bear rushed in and
dived under the bed. But there
wasn't a monster, just a stinky old sock.

Big Bear put his hand in the sock and made stinky sock monster noises.

Then he bundled Little Bear back into bed.
"Night, night, don't let the bed socks
bite!" chuckled Big Bear.

Little Bear snuggled down and tried to go to sleep,
but he felt lost in the middle of his big new bed.
It was just too lonely without Big Bear there.
Little Bear's lip started to wobble and he was just
about to cry when he heard footsteps coming closer.

Tip, tap!

Tip, tap!

The door slowly opened . . .

It was **Big Bear!**

"There's no need to be frightened, Little Bear," he said.

"But I don't like being all on my own," sniffed Little Bear.

"Don't worry," said Big Bear, "I've brought Old Hoppity to keep you company."

He tucked his favourite, tattered toy into bed with Little Bear. "Now you won't feel so scared," he said.

"Silly Little Bear," chuckled
Big Bear, as he went back to bed.
"Frightened of monsters!"

Big Bear snuggled down in his bed and tried to
go to sleep . . . but he couldn't. His bedroom
seemed so empty without Little Bear there.
Big Bear lay in the dark, humming a
little song to keep the quiet out.
Just then, he heard a noise,
a growly, snuffling noise . . .

. . . and it was coming from
Little Bear's bedroom!

Snurffle!

Snort!

"OH NO!" thought Big Bear. "Maybe there really
IS a stinky sock monster under the bed and it wants
a little bear for its supper!"

Big Bear raced down the hallway as the noises
got louder and louder.

Snurffle,

Snurffle!

Snort,

snort!

"I'll save you, Little Bear!" he cried,
pushing open the door . . .

But there wasn't a **stinky sock monster!** Just a small bear, fast asleep and

snoring loudly

in the growly, snuffly way that little bears do.